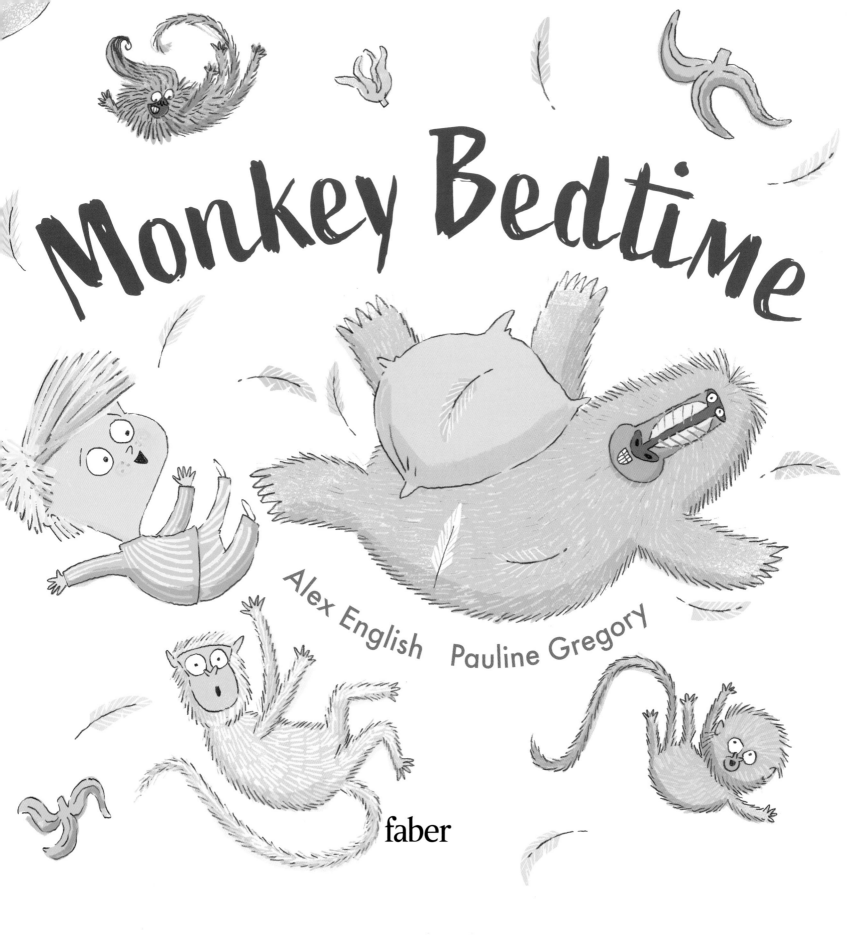

Monkey Bedtime

Alex English   Pauline Gregory

faber

For Freddie
and George, A.E.

Especially for Ryan,
you're one of a kind.
All my love, P.G.

First published in the UK in 2022
First published in the US in 2022
by Faber and Faber Limited
Bloomsbury House,
74–77 Great Russell Street,
London WC1B 3DA
faberchildrens.co.uk
Text © Alex English, 2022
Illustrations © Pauline Gregory, 2022
Designed by Faber and Faber
HB ISBN 978-0-571-35276-0
PB ISBN 978-0-571-35277-7

The moral rights of Alex English and Pauline Gregory have been asserted
A CIP record for this book is available from the British Library

Faber has published children's books since 1929. T. S. Eliot's *Old Possum's Book of Practical Cats* and Ted Hughes' *The Iron Man* were amongst the first. Our catalogue at the time said that 'it is by reading such books that children learn the difference between the shoddy and the genuine'. We still believe in the power of reading to transform children's lives. All our books are chosen with the express intention of growing a love of reading, a thirst for knowledge and to cultivate empathy. We pride ourselves on responsible editing. Last but not least, we believe in kind and inclusive books in which all children feel represented and important.

The sky was dark. The moon was bright.

'It's bedtime,' Mommy said.

So I grabbed my book
and teddy bear and
ran upstairs to bed.

But suddenly I heard an EEK, a TAP TAP on the pane.
A tiny little monkey face was peering through the rain.

I'm sure my mom won't mind, I thought. He's really very small.
One tiny pygmy marmoset could do no harm at all . . .

. . . so I let him in the window, and we **bounced** on all the beds.

We counted stars and raced my cars and balanced on

our

heads!

'It's bedtime,' called my mommy. 'Please come and wash your face.'
But the marmoset swung down the stairs and off I ran in chase.

Then he opened up the door and let a load MORE monkeys in.
There were six red-handed howlers and a lion tamarin!

'It's time for bed,' I told them, as they turned on the TV.
But they shrieked and pulled rude faces, threw banana skins at me.

The howler monkeys giggled as they climbed the curtain rails,
then they hollered, howled and hiccupped
as they hung there by their tails.

'Please brush your teeth,' yelled Mommy,
'and who's making all that noise?'

'I'm coming, Mom,' I shouted back.
'Just tidying my toys.'

But sailing down the chimney came a mandrill with balloons,
and six macaques, ten capuchins and two great big baboons.

'No more!' I told the monkeys,
but they screamed, 'AH-AH-OOH!'
as they scampered to the bathroom
and guzzled Mom's shampoo.

The tamarin burped out his name
in bubbles in the air.

The marmoset jumped in the sink, squeezed toothpaste in his hair.

'Where are your pajamas? It is BEDTIME!' Mommy said.
'No MORE!' I begged the monkey mob. 'I have to go to bed!'

But the monkeys didn't listen. They whooped, 'OOH-AH-AH-OOH!'

Then they opened up the window and three gibbons came in, too!

'To the kitchen!' shrieked the mandrill,
and they scampered down the stairs.

The howler monkeys juggled with the pineapples and pears.

The capuchins left little jelly handprints *up* the *wall.*

'Oh, these monkeys are big trouble. Mom will not like this at all!'

'It's bedtime,' shouted Mommy. 'What is going on down there?'
'In a minute, Mom,' I yelled. 'I've lost my teddy bear!'

I turned around to look, and then I let out quite a wail.
One baboon slurped jelly and dripped ice cream from its tail.

A big macaque did backflips with my underwear on its ears.

The gibbons grinned and giggled, but MY eyes filled up with tears.

The house was in a monkey jumble, messy as could be.
I cried, 'NO MORE, YOU SILLY MONKEYS,
OR MY MOMMY WILL BLAME ME!'

And

every

monkey

stopped.

Suddenly the monkey mob grew quiet as a mouse.
They shivered and they quivered as they looked around the house.

'Oh, please don't cry! We're sorry
and we don't want any trouble!
We'll tidy up this mess at once;
we'll clean it on the double!'

So the gibbons wiped the windows and the mandrill took a broom,
And they cleaned and scrubbed and swept until they'd tidied every room.

The bedroom,

lounge

and
bathroom,

and the kitchen counters, too.

Then I heard the mandrill whisper,
'Quick, let's get back to the zoo!'

And then they disappeared, as if I had been dreaming.
And the house was so tidy, it was sparkling and gleaming.

So I put on my pajama pants and tumbled into bed.
'What a lot of monkeying around!' my mommy said.

But when she went downstairs, she grinned and cried, 'Well done!
What a tidy house! I'm so proud of you, my son.

As an extra-special treat I'll take you out to the zoo.
I know you love the monkeys. There's a tea party at two!'

MONKEY TEA
PARTY TODAY
AT 2 PM